# EARTHQUAKES

A TRUE BOOK

by

## Paul P. Sipiera

Children's Press®
A Division of Grolier Publishing
New York  London  Hong Kong  Sydney
Danbury, Connecticut

*Reading Consultant*
**Linda Cornwell**
*Learning Resource Consultant*
*Indiana Department*
*of Education*

**Author's Dedication**
*To Mike McDowell,*
*a good friend and*
*a real mover and shaker*

Earthquake-damaged
apartments

**Visit Children's Press® on the Internet at:**
http://publishing.grolier.com

Library of Congress Cataloging-in-Publication Data

Sipiera, Paul P.
    Earthquakes / by Paul P. Sipiera.
        p.    cm. — (A true book)
    Includes bibliographical references and index.
    Summary: Introduces the origins, causes, and destructive effects of earthquakes.
    ISBN: 0-516-20665-6 (lib.bdg.)       0-516-26432-X (pbk.)
    1. Earthquakes—Juvenile literature.   [1.  Earthquakes.] I.  Title.
    II.  Series.
        QE521.3.S57    1998
        551.22—dc21                                                         97-34930
                                                                                CIP
                                                                                AC

# Contents

# Earth

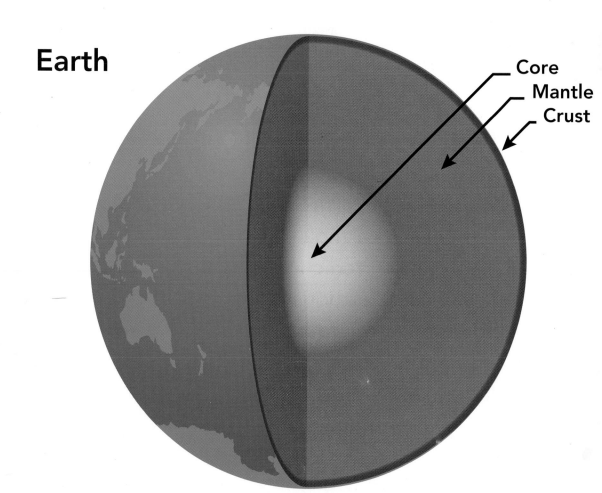

Core
Mantle
Crust

A view of Earth's core, mantle, and crust

# Deep Inside Earth

Earth is divided into three parts: the crust, the mantle, and the core. The crust forms Earth's surface. It is made of many different kinds of rock. Basalt is a dark-colored volcanic rock. It makes up the crust under the oceans. On land, the most common rock is called

The layers that make up sedimentary rock can be seen throughout the Grand Canyon in Arizona.

sedimentary (sed-uh-MEN-tuh-ree). This type of rock is made up of bits and pieces of other rocks.

Beneath the crust is the mantle. This is where many earthquakes begin. Here, temperatures are very hot. The heat causes some of the rock to soften. This softened rock is called magma. It is similar to "silly putty." It changes shape slowly. Magma moves through the mantle in a circular motion. The hottest magma rises toward Earth's surface. The cooler magma sinks farther into the mantle.

Magma rises toward Earth's crust through convection.

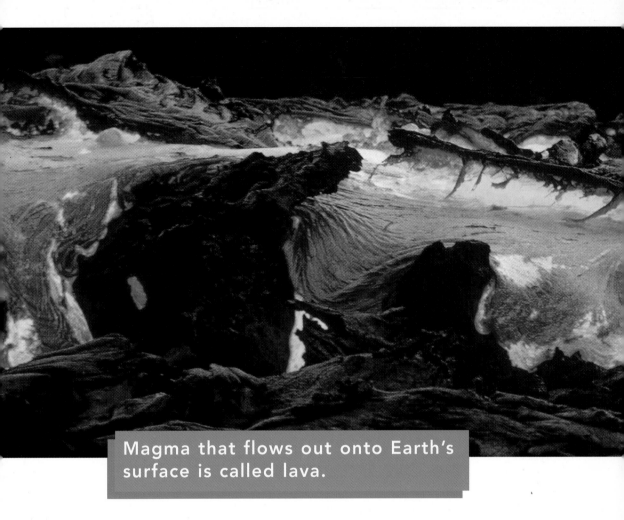

Magma that flows out onto Earth's surface is called lava.

This process is called convection (kuhn-VEK-shuhn). The circular movement of magma is the force behind earthquakes.

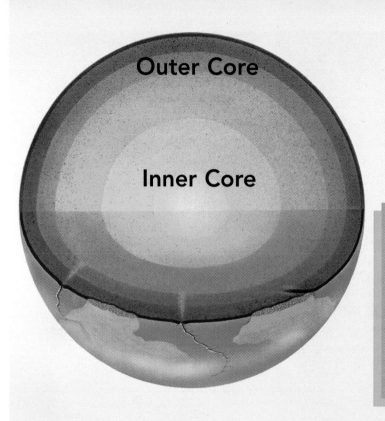

Outer Core

Inner Core

The bright-yellow area illustrates Earth's inner, solid core. The yellowish-orange area illustrates Earth's outer, liquid core.

Below the mantle is Earth's core. The core has two parts. One part is liquid. It is made up of melted metals. This part of the core is a little larger than the Moon. The other part of the core is made up of solid metals.

# Earth's Plates

Earth's crust is broken into big sections called plates. These plates fit together like pieces of a puzzle. They are similar to big rafts floating on the ocean. Convection within the mantle causes the plates to move. Earthquakes are common at the edges of some plates.

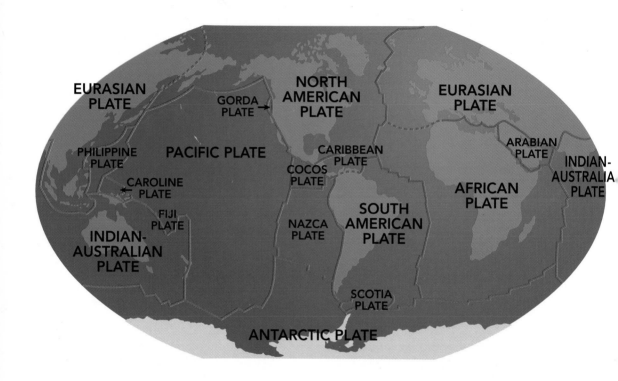

Each year, Earth's plates move at about the same rate as your fingernails grow.

There are about ten large plates and about twenty smaller ones. The names of a few of the biggest plates are: the Pacific Plate, the North American Plate, the Antarctic Plate, and the African Plate. The United States is located on the North American Plate.

Some of the smaller plates have names such as: the Caribbean Plate, the Cocos Plate, the Gorda Plate, and the Fiji Plate.

# What Makes Earth Shake?

As magma circulates, the force of the circular motion pulls the crust apart. When this happens, it can leave a gap, or space, in Earth's crust. This gap is called a fault. A fault marks a weak spot where an earthquake can occur.

This earthquake fault runs through Tashkent, the capital of Uzbekistan.

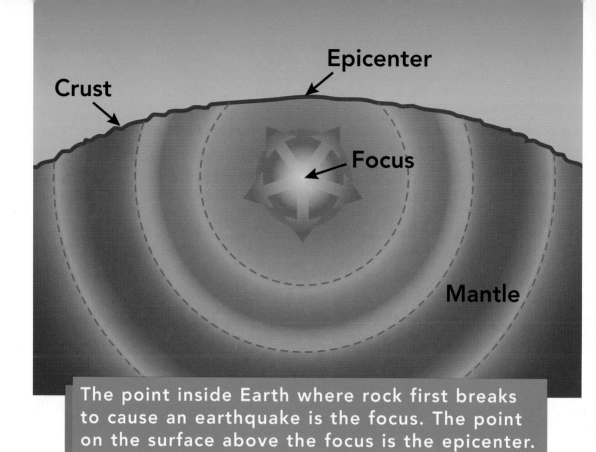

Crust

Epicenter

Focus

Mantle

The point inside Earth where rock first breaks to cause an earthquake is the focus. The point on the surface above the focus is the epicenter.

Every earthquake has two parts. One part is called the focus. The focus is the spot inside Earth where an earth-quake occurs. The second part is called the epicenter (EP-uh-sent-ur). The epicenter is the point on Earth's surface that lies directly above the focus. The area around the epicenter is in the most danger during an earthquake.

When an earthquake strikes, the ground shakes. Buildings sway back and forth. Other structures may bounce up and down. Sometimes houses are bounced right off their foundations. In 1989, an earthquake

Workers check the damage to part of the two-level freeway that collapsed in Oakland, California, in October 1989.

hit the San Francisco Bay area of California. The top level of a two-level freeway collapsed onto the bottom level.

18

# The San Andreas Fault

The San Andreas fault is located in California. It is 600 miles (970 kilometers) long and marks a spot where two plates meet. One plate is the Pacific Plate. The other plate is the North American Plate. When the plates slip a little, an earthquake occurs.

# Dangerous Earthquakes

Scientists developed two scales to describe earthquakes. A scale is a series of numbers that is used to measure an earthquake's power. The two most widely used scales are the Mercalli scale and the Richter scale. Each scale describes the damage that is

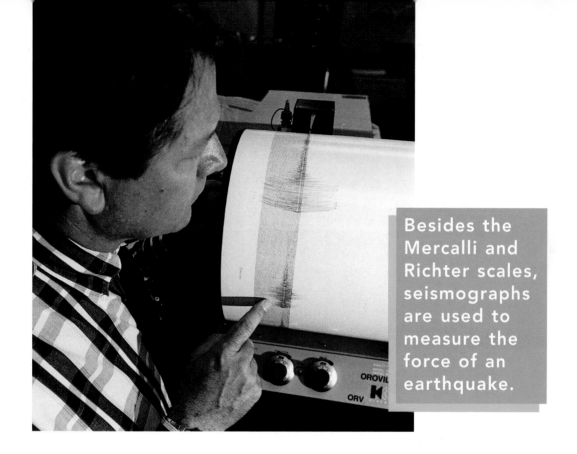

Besides the Mercalli and Richter scales, seismographs are used to measure the force of an earthquake.

produced by an earthquake. The Richter scale is used more often than the Mercalli scale. The Richter scale refers to the magnitude, or size, of an earthquake. The scale

Anchorage, Alaska, after the 1964 earthquake that measured 8.4 on the Richter scale

begins with the number 1. The higher the number is on the scale, the greater the damage an earthquake has caused. An earthquake that measures 3 or 4 doesn't cause as much damage as an earthquake of 5 or 6.

Buildings, such as this one in Mexico, can be severly damaged when they are built on unsafe ground.

The power of an earth-quake is not the only cause of damage to an area. Buildings that are built on loose gravel or on sand usually suffer the

Workers search for survivors following an earthquake in Mexico City.

greatest damage because the
ground is not firm. Poorly con-
structed buildings are another
reason people are killed in

earthquakes. If the buildings are not strong, they can collapse on top of the people inside.

Major earthquakes can cause great damage and loss of life. But many more lives can be lost during aftershocks. Aftershocks are a series of smaller earthquakes that follow a big earthquake. Aftershocks often occur as rescue workers are searching for victims in damaged buildings.

After an earthquake destroyed this man's southern California home (above), the house had to be completely rebuilt. In 1995, citizens left the city of Kobe, Japan (right), because it was unsafe after a serious earthquake.

The buildings can then easily collapse on the victims and the rescuers. The time directly following an earthquake can be quite dangerous.

Fire is another problem that can follow an earthquake. An earthquake can break natural gas pipelines and damage water pipes. The leaking gas easily catches fire. If water pipes are damaged, there may be little or no water to put out the flames. Buildings and

The fires that sometimes occur after an earthquake strikes can threaten survivors' lives.

sections of a city that weren't destroyed by the earthquake can be destroyed by the fire that follows.

An earthquake that takes place beneath the ocean can create a huge wall of seawater called a tsunami (tsoo-NAH-mee). Tsunami is a Japanese

Tuna remain in a street on an island in Indonesia after a tsunami swept through the town in 1992.

Tsunami
100 feet
(30 meters) high

Adult
6 feet
(183 centimeters) ta

A 6-foot (183-centimeter)-tall adult
looks tiny compared to the 100-foot
(30-meter) height of a tsunami.

word that means "harbor wave." Tsunamis can reach heights of more than 100 feet (30 meters). They can travel at speeds of 300 to 600 miles (500 to 950 kilometers) per hour. When a tsunami hits the shore, it can wash away everything in its path. Sometimes, people who are thousands of miles away from an earthquake can be killed by the tsunami it created.

# Earthquake Facts

Here are some interesting facts about earthquakes that you may not know:

The most powerful earthquake ever recorded in North America occurred in 1811 in Missouri. It was so powerful that it caused the Mississippi River to flow backward for three days.

The Mississippi River

The most powerful earthquake ever recorded on Earth occurred in Chile (South America) in 1960. It measured 9.5 on the Richter scale.

A man in front of the rubble of his business after the 1960 earthquake in Chile

Sometimes smaller earthquakes occur before the big earthquake hits. They are called foreshocks. Foreshocks can occur minutes, hours, or days before the main earthquake.

Most people don't realize that foreshocks have taken place.

The amount of time that Earth shakes during an earthquake can last from a few seconds to three or four minutes.

This apartment building in California shook back and forth for about thirty seconds.

# Earthquake Prediction

Scientists have tried to predict, or to know in advance, when an earthquake will occur. But predicting an earthquake is extremely difficult. Only one major earthquake has been successfully predicted. It occurred in 1975 in China. Three million people were evacuated from a

This scientist is measuring earthquake activity near a fault. He is working on a way to predict earthquakes.

city just hours before an earthquake destroyed it.

Scientists use many different methods to predict earthquakes. However, none of the methods has been too successful. One of the most common ways that scientists try to predict earthquakes is by studying a fault. The scientists also look for a pattern in the number of earthquakes that have occurred over a certain amount of time. Unfortunately, these predictions cannot give the exact date and time of the next earthquake.

Some people believe that nature has its own way of predicting an earthquake. Just before an earthquake strikes,

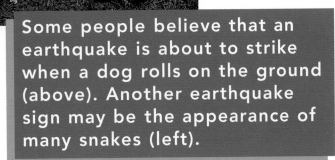

Some people believe that an earthquake is about to strike when a dog rolls on the ground (above). Another earthquake sign may be the appearance of many snakes (left).

people may see animals acting strangely and snakes coming out of the ground. Water levels in wells might change. When all of these signs occur at the same time, it is thought that an earthquake is about to strike.

Earthquake predictions can help to save lives by giving people a chance to leave an area and find safety. But there is also danger in earthquake predictions. Once a warning is given, people often panic. This can result in more people being killed fleeing a city than if they remain there through the earthquake.

Another danger happens if an earthquake is predicted, but does not occur. The next time a warning is given, the people might not listen to the scientists.

The people living in this house were able to evacuate to safety before the earthquake struck.

# Living with Earthquakes

Many areas of the world have experienced major earthquakes. In the United States, Alaska and both northern and southern California have had devastating earthquakes. Japan, Mexico, Russia, and other countries have also suffered great destruction. No place on Earth

This apartment house in San Francisco, California, was three stories high before an earthquake flattened it. Supports (left) keep it from toppling into the street.

is totally safe from earthquakes. But some places have more earthquakes than others.

In some dangerous earth-quake areas, there is little that people can do to protect them-selves. One thing they can do is construct buildings that will withstand all but the most pow-erful earthquakes. It is also important to keep hospitals, hotels, and other public buildings away from dangerous faults. This can lessen the loss of life and property. Once people learn how to live with earthquakes, their cities will become safer places.

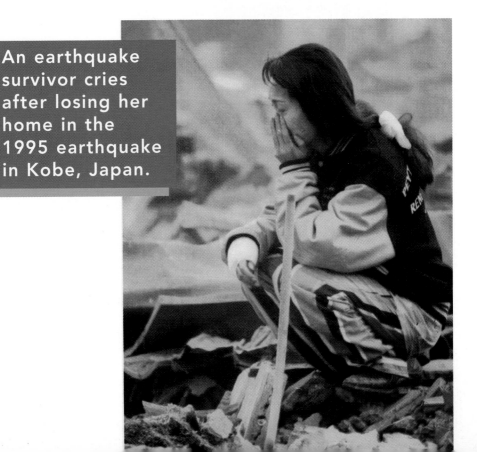

An earthquake survivor cries after losing her home in the 1995 earthquake in Kobe, Japan.

# To Find Out More

Here are some additional resources to help you learn more about earthquakes:

 **Books**

Branley, Franklyn M.
**Earthquakes.**
HarperCollins Children's
Books, 1994.

Gold, Stephen and Maria
Gold. **Earthquakes!**
Humanics Ltd., 1992.

Lye, Keith. **Earthquakes.**
Raintree Steck-Vaughn,
1996.

Murray, Peter.
**Earthquakes.** Child's
World, 1995.

Simon, Seymour.
**Earthquakes.** Morrow
Junior Books, 1991.

# Organizations and Online Sites

## United States Geological Survey (USGS)
804 National Center
Reston, VA 20192
*http://www.usgs.gov*

## Ask-A-Geologist
*http://www.walrus.wr.usgs.gov*

Do you have a question about earthquakes? You can e-mail your question to a scientist at the USGS! This site also contains sample questions and answers, as well as links to other sites.

## Earthquakes
*http://www.Science/Earth_Sciences/Geology_and_Geophysics/Seismology/*

This site connects you to related earthquake sites, including earthquake prediction, tsunamis, and daily and weekly earthquake updates.

## Earth Science
*http://www.sci.geo.earthquakes*

Try this site for more on how earthquakes occur, illustrations, maps, answers to questions, and links to related sites.

## What's Shakin' in California?
*http://www.ca.earthquakes*

A lot of information and statistics about earthquakes that have occurred in California.

# Important Words

*evacuate* to move away from an area
because it is dangerous

*foundation* solid structure on which a
building is built

*freeway* wide highway used for travel

*magma* hot liquid below Earth's surface that will cool and form rock

*magnitude* number used to indicate
the power of an earthquake

*pipeline* line of large pipes that carry
water, gas, or oil over long dis-
tances

# Index

# Meet the Author

Paul P. Sipiera is a professor of geology and astronomy at William Rainey Harper College in Palatine, Illinois. His main areas of research are in meteorites and volcanic rocks.

He is a member of the Explorers Club, the New Zealand Antarctic Society, and serves as president of the Planetary Studies Foundation. When he is not studying science, he can be found working his small farm in Galena, Illinois, with his wife Diane and their three daughters Andrea, Paula Frances, and Caroline Antarctica.

Photographs ©: AP/Wide World Photos: 33 top (John Fung), 26 bottom (Katsumi Kasaha), 26 top (Douglas C. Pizac), 18 (Paul Sakuma), 32 bottom (William J. Smith), 21 (Walt Zeboski), cover, 43; Archive Photos: 22; Bernard Adnet: 4, 12, 16, 30; Corbis-Bettmann: 1 (Chris Wilkins/AFP); Photo Researchers: 8 (George Chan), 37 bottom (Francois Gohier), 10 (David Hardy/SPL), 37 top (John Kaprielian), 15 (Fred McConnaughey), 9 (Stephen and Donna O'Meara), 33 bottom (David Weintraub); Reuters/Archive Photos: 42 (David Brauchli), 29 (Enny Nuraheni), 28 (John Pryke), 24 (Paul Richards); Tom Bean: 6, 19; Tony Stone Images: 32 top (Nathan Benn), 2 (Leverett Bradley), 41 (Bruce Hands), 39 (Kevin Schafer), 23 (Robert Yager).